More Spooky Texas Tales

More Spooky Texas Tales

Tim Tingle and Doc Moore
Illustrated by Jeanne A. Benas

Texas Tech University Press

This book is typeset in Sabon. The paper used in this book meets the mini-
mum requirements of ANSI/NISO Z39.48-1992 (R1997).

Designed by Kasey McBeath

Library of Congress Cataloging-in-Publication Data
Tingle, Tim.
    More spooky Texas tales / Tim Tingle and Doc Moore ; illustrated by
Jeanne A. Benas.
        v. cm.
    Contents: La Llorona at Mission Concepción — Mary Culhaine — Skin-
walker — The Gypsy drum — The woman with cat's eyes — The monkey's
paw — Screaming banshee cattle of the night swamp — Chupacabra — Catfish and the owl — Two graves.
    ISBN 978-0-89672-700-7 (lithocase : alk. paper) 1. Ghost stories, Ameri-
can. 2. Children's stories, American. [1. Horror stories. 2. Texas—Fiction. 3.
Short stories.] I. Moore, Doc. II. Benas, Jeanne A., ill. III. Title.
    PZ7.T489Mo 2010
    [Fic]—dc22   2010016568

Printed in the United States of America

16 17 18 / 9 8 7 6 5 4 3 2

Texas Tech University Press
Box 41037 | Lubbock, Texas 79409-1037 USA
800.832.4042 | ttup@ttu.edu | www.ttupress.org

To Beth Dewey,
teacher and friend

Contents

✳ Acknowledgments

*I*n our previous ghost stories books, we have given thanks to our storytelling friends, but for *More Spooky Texas Tales* we must render our gratitude to students. For years elementary and middle school students have entertained us with their favorite ghostly tales. We have been awestruck by student tellings of La Llorona, the weeping woman of Spanish lore, and of the Chupacabra, the blood-sucking wolf creature from the Rio Grande Valley.

"Skinwalker" was a gift from a young Navajo boy we met during a school performance. My own son Jacob, as an elementary student, cringed and squiggled for years as we drove across the Louisiana swamp country and I warned him of the "Screaming Banshee Cattle of the Night Swamp."

Immense thanks to Greg Rodgers, fellow Choctaw writer, for inspiring "Two Graves," based on his memory of an old newspaper article, and "Catfish and the Owl," which incorporates elements of Choctaw tribal lore.

Doc Moore and I always enjoy Gay Ducey's eerily beautiful telling of "The Gypsy Drum," and Irish-Texan teller John Burleson's "Mary Culhaine," and wanted to include our versions in this volume. Many modern storytellers tell "The Monkey's Paw"; the version here is Doc Moore's East Texas variation. Dr. John Davis of the Institute of Texas Cultures tells a horrifying story, "The Cat's Eyes," from Spanish folklore. Doc Moore and I created a suburban tale based on the same motif, "The Woman with Cat's Eyes." Thanks to all students: this book is yours!

Tim Tingle

More Spooky Texas Tales

La Llorona at Mission Concepción

Many people say that La Llorona, the Weeping Woman, is the best-known ghost in the world. Children are warned of her at a very early age. Some say La Llorona haunts the riverbanks after dark, looking for her lost children and luring other children to the water, to be with her.

One beautiful Sunday afternoon in June, many years ago, a wedding took place at Mission Concepción in San Antonio. Hundreds of family and friends were gathered. Among the wedding guests were two young cousins of the bride, Cheo and his older sister, Juanita.

After the wedding, the celebration moved onto the mission grounds for music and feasting. With no friends or cousins their age, Juanita and Cheo grew bored and grumpy.

"You look like an old woman at a funeral," said Cheo, pulling the scarf from his sister's head.

"Keep the scarf if you need it," said Juanita. "Why don't you wear it? You look like a clown already."

Cheo felt like a clown. His pants were six inches too long and

3

his sleeves hung over his hands. "Oh yeah!" he yelled at Juanita, wadding her scarf and throwing it back at her.

"Yeah, silly boy," she said, retying the scarf over her head. "Did the wicked witch shrink you or were you born too small for your clothes?"

Soon their mother saw them fighting. "You children are embarrassing me," she said. "I never see my family. Don't you want to sit with us at the table," she said, pointing to a long wooden table under a clump of trees. Two dozen people were passing platters of food and pitchers of icy lemonade.

"We want to go home," said Cheo.

"We don't know these people," said Juanita.

"Of course you do! They are your family," said their mother. "I'll get your great aunt Marta. She can take you to the park."

"I don't even know her," Juanita protested.

Her mother disappeared into the crowd, and within a few minutes a small elderly woman approached the children.

"Follow me," she said, and they did, crossing the dirt road and walking along the nearby riverbank. They walked for almost a mile till the old woman spread her *rebozo* on the ground. In the soft grass and shade of the cottonwood trees, she motioned for the children to join her.

"I don't want to sit down," said Cheo. "I want to go swimming!" He took off his shoes and dashed to the river.

"You better stop or I'll tell mother," said Juanita.

"She won't care."

"You get that suit dirty and you'll see how much she cares," said Juanita. Cheo made a face and returned to the bank, but the children continued bickering. Finally, the old woman had enough. She clapped her hands.

"¡Siléncio, niños! La Llorona would know what to do with children such as you!" she shouted.

Cheo and Juanita fell silent. Their eyes grew large. They knew of La Llorona, the weeping woman who haunted the riverbanks after dark. The old woman, now that she had their attention, began her story.

"Maria was her name. She was born to a poor family, but they were good people. Much like you, Juanita, she was very beautiful, even as a child. But she was *orgullosa*! Pride filled her heart. She walked with her nose in the air.

"One Sunday afternoon as she was shopping with her mother, a wealthy young man spotted Maria. He was taken by her beauty. As they moved from stall to stall in the crowded market, he would not let Maria from his sight. He even followed them home that evening to see where Maria lived.

"One day he appeared at her doorstep.

"'May I speak with Maria?' he asked her mother. He was allowed to enter, and the two sat quietly under the watchful eye of Maria's mother and two aunts. After many visits and months of courtship, Maria and the young man were married.

"They had two children. The first was a beautiful little girl. The second was a boy as handsome as you, Cheo.

"Maria loved her children deeply, as did the young man. But his family was very rich and lived hundreds of miles away. The man soon grew tired of life among the poor. One day he told Maria, 'I am going to see my family. You take care of the children and I will be back in a month.'

"Maria was left alone with the children. The young man did not return, not after a month, not even after a year. But one day Maria spotted him, walking among the stalls at the marketplace, where he had first seen her. He was walking with a young woman dressed in expensive clothing.

"Maria felt the stares and heard the gossip of the stallkeepers as she moved, eyes downcast, through the marketplace. A black cloud seemed to follow her."

The old woman then tilted her head back, closed her eyes, and reached out for the children.

"Cheo! Juanita! Come close to me. This is a sad story with an ugly ending, and I am an old woman alone in the world."

"There are many versions of the story. In one, Maria leaves the marketplace in a fury, calls to her children, and tells them, 'Come to me.' She takes them to the riverbank and drowns them to punish their father.

"They say she still wanders up and down the banks of the rivers, calling for her children, crying for her lost children. They also say she is looking for children, any children, alone by the river at night. Who knows what she will do when she finds them?"

The old woman closed her eyes and slowly shook her head. When she once again looked upon the children, it was as if she was returning from a dream.

"My little one. May I call you Little Cheo? You can be my little one for a while. Would that be all right?"

Cheo nodded and the old woman began to rock. Little Cheo fell asleep in her arms. Juanita, too, stretched out in the tall grass and slept. The old woman continued talking to herself.

Shortly after dark, Juanita awoke and discovered she was alone. She hurried back to the church, expecting to find her Aunt Marta and Cheo. What she found were hundreds of people in an uproar, frantically searching for her and her brother.

"Juanita, my precious Juanita!" her mother cried. "Where is your brother?"

"He is with Aunt Marta," said Juanita. "We were napping down by the river."

Her mother looked confused.

"But Juanita, Marta and I have been looking for you all afternoon. You have not been with her."

"Then who was the old woman who took us to the river?" asked Juanita. A dozen men, holding their lanterns before them, ran in the direction of the river, calling, "Cheo! Cheo!"

As they moved near the water, they heard a piercing wail from the opposite shore. "¡Hijos, hijos! ¿Dónde están mis hijos? Where are my children?"

The searchers halted. They threw themselves to the ground in fear while Juanita ran with her mother to the river. There she saw Cheo, clinging to a bush on the riverbank, his feet already in the water. The old woman seemed to float above the water, smiling and reaching for him.

"Help me! Juanita, help me!" he called.

Juanita ran to the river, then froze in her tracks. She saw three children in the water, their faces below the surface.

"Ghost children!" she shouted. The children smiled dark smiles and grabbed Cheo. A young boy held him by the legs and the others clutched at his shirt tail. The fog thickened, and Juanita saw only a thick cloud of mist before her eyes. From the mist came an eerie sound, a chorus of voices whispering, "¡Hijos! ¡Hijos!"

Twenty more children suddenly appeared, crying from the river, crying till their shouts filled the foggy air for miles, screaming and pulling on Cheo. His hands slipped from the branches, one by one, and his fingers left thin mud trails on the

7

riverbank as he slid beneath the water.

"NO!" shouted Juanita. "No! You cannot have my brother!"

The children cast their eyes at her, and the smiles left their faces. Juanita leapt into the river and wrapped her arms around Cheo's waist. She pulled hard—only once, but that was enough. The ghostly children slowly vanished and their cries grew weak. Juanita pulled Cheo to the bank. The fog lifted and several of his uncles rushed him to the safety of the church.

Years later, one fine and beautiful Sunday in June, Juanita was married at Mission Concepción. She had two children. The second was a son and she named him Cheo, after her brother, whom she dearly loved. When Uncle Cheo came to visit, she often told the children of how he almost drowned.

"What happened to La Llorona?" they always asked him.

"Your brave mother was stronger. The Weeping Woman knew better than to stay in San Antonio!" Uncle Cheo always said.

Mary Culhaine

If he'd known what would happen to his young daughter Mary, Mr. Culhaine would never have allowed her to go to the graveyard after dark. But he had no way of knowing and neither did she, so the story's been told for centuries about what happened that night to Mary Culhaine.

I didn't want to come home late, so I took the shortcut through the graveyard," said Mister Culhaine to his wife that night. "I accidentally left my walking cane. It's lying there against an old gray tombstone."

"I'll get it for you," said Mary, for she loved her father dearly.

"It's too dark!" called her mother, but Mary was already gone.

She found the cane easily enough. She gripped it tight, but when she turned, something was gripping her. It held her by the wrist and it was strong. Mary jerked and wriggled as only a deathly terrified young girl can. Then, bracing her feet against the stone, she leaned all her weight the other way and fell to the ground.

At first she was relieved. You would be, too. But the thing still held her by the wrist, and now she got a look at it. Light as a bundle of wheat and skinny as death it was, which should come as a surprise to nobody, because of course the thing was dead.

Dry skin hung in patches from his neck and face and even his shinbones. Trust me, he was hideously ugly. Sprouts of scraggly hair clung to his skull and his teeth were black, what few were there. Deep, dark circles were all that remained of his eyes.

Then the thing, hunched over and crooked at the spine, flung itself upon her back. He dug his bony heels into her ribs, grabbed her by the neck and nose, and screamed into her ears.

"Walk, little girl. Take me to town!"

"My name is Mary, not little girl," said Mary.

"Oh, pleased to meet you, Mary," said the thing, digging his heels deeper into her ribs. "And what would your last name be?"

"Mary Culhaine," said you-know-who.

"Well, pleased to meet you, Mary Culhaine," said the thing, in a sweet cooing voice. "Now, you hag of a little girl, take me to town!"

Mary thought to herself, *He might be ugly and dead already, but at least he still has manners.* And what could she do? She did the same as you or I would do. She took him into town. He pointed with his bony arm and finger and said, "Take me in that house. I'm hungry."

But when they came up to the house, he covered his eyes and squalled, "No, Mary, I can't go there."

"Why not?" asked Mary.

"The people are too old there. Their blood flows slow, and I want warm, young blood," said the thing. Mary shivered to

11

hear it. She knew she'd be expected to serve him, and she couldn't imagine how he'd want the blood to be cooked. She wished she had her cookbook.

He pointed to another house and hollered louder than before. "Take me there. I want to eat!" Mary Culhaine stopped. He was looking at her house. She tried not moving, but she couldn't help herself. She walked up to her door.

And then he screamed and covered his eyes like they were burning.

"Oh, no, we cannot enter here. There's cat hair on the doorstep!"

Picky, picky, picky, thought Mary, but she knew better than to say it. She loved her cat and liked him best with his blood still flowing.

Finally, he pointed to a third house, and when they stepped up to the porch, she saw him smile. At least she thought she did. But since his face had no lips, she couldn't really know. They entered the house and stepped into the kitchen. "Make oatmeal, Mary. I'm hungry for it," the thing said.

"They'll hear us in the house," she said.

"They'll never know it, Mary. Just cook it, now!"

She didn't want to, but she did. When the oatmeal bubbled hot and thick, he grabbed the pot. "There are boys upstairs, three of them," he said.

"I don't think so," she said, lying, for she knew the boys. They were teenage boys, but all polite and nice to her.

"Well, I think so," he said. "Up the stairs you go."

So Mary Culhaine with the awful dead thing on her back walked up the stairs.

The boys all stayed in one bedroom, sleeping with their hands and arms hanging over the bed. The smelly dead thing pulled a knife, a tiny sharp one. He cackled and made her stoop to the first boy.

"Lean over, Mary, you haggy little girl, and lift his arm."

He sliced the end of the boy's finger off and caught it in the pot. Then he caught the blood that flowed. When the first drop fell, the boy grew cold. With the second drop, his face turned blue. When the third drop fell, the boy's heart stopped. He lay there dead as a rock.

"All right and to the next," he said. Drop by bloody drop he drained the life from those three boys. When the oatmeal pot was bloody and hardly looking like a meal, he said, "I must eat, Mary, time is short. Quick, down the stairs and to the table, for we'll eat civilized."

Once again, thought Mary, *he demonstrates his manners.*

Finally, for her ribs were growing weary of his bony feet, the old dead thing crawled off her back and took a chair.

"Two bowls!" he said, and Mary did it quickly. He spooned her bowl as full as his own.

"Now, eat!"

Mary wasn't hungry, but his ugly eye was on her. She filled her spoon and lifted it. The old thing put his head down in the bloody bowl and sucked the oatmeal through his teeth, the few teeth that remained. It made an awful slurping sound.

So Mary saw her chance. She scooped the oatmeal spoon by spoon until her bowl was empty. She put it in her scarf. When the old man saw her bowl had nothing in it, he laughed a horrid hissing sound.

"Are the boys forever dead?" Mary asked.

"Forever and always," hissed the thing. "Only a taste of the bloody oatmeal would bring them back to life. Now you've gone and eaten it all! Too bad! Besides all that, you're one of us," he wheezed and giggled. "Take me to the graveyard and be quick. Day is coming. It's the end of me if the sun should ever shine on these old dried-out bones."

They crossed a rocky haunted field. The old man pulled her hair and said, "You see that pile of rocks, Mary? All of us that haunt these graves, we keep our treasure there."

"Why are you telling me this?" said Mary.

"Why, Mary, don't you know? You've eaten of the blood and now you're one of us."

He leapt from her back and pulled her to the grave where she had seen him first. His toes wiggled and curled and he sank into the grave. It was a gory thing to see. He was strong now from the blood.

If the sun had not come over the hill and struck the dead man on his face, I don't know what would have happened. But it did.

"Mary, look at me," he cried, and then he turned to ashes and was gone.

Mary walked straightaway back to the boys' house. Everyone in town was there and saying, "They've all been murdered."

"Well, I would like to see them all alone," said Mary. They led her to the room and closed the door. She took the oatmeal from her scarf and fed them, one by one. One by one their lives returned.

The end of it all was that Mary Culhaine never had to work from that day on, and neither did her father or her mother. They always seemed to have plenty of money. If they walked at night, it was never near the graveyard. Never again did they go that way, not even for a walking cane.

Skinwalker

We were camping on the banks of the Rio Grande River, my dad and my friends, Roland and Gary, when a young boy, maybe eight, stepped from the mesquite bushes and asked if he could have a drink of water.

"Sure," said dad. "We have Cokes if you'd rather have one."

"A Coke will be good," said the boy, smiling.

"Do you live nearby?" asked my dad.

"Across the river," the boy said. We all nodded as if that explained everything.

We had been telling dumb jokes, but somehow it seemed rude to start "knock, knock, who's there"-ing again. So we sat without saying anything, which I guess was even more rude. But what do you say?

The boy finished his Coke and stood to go.

"You are welcome anytime," said my dad. Then he laughed and said something that made me very proud. "I guess that is a funny thing to be doing, welcoming you. After all, this is your home, not ours."

The boy nodded a slow nod of understanding and respect. "But you have built the fire," he said, "and shared a drink with me. You seem like nice people. Do you know about Skin-walker?"

"No," we all seemed to say at once. The boy said nothing for a long minute, then sat near the fire. "I should tell you about Skinwalker, so you will not end up like that man from Alabama. You are not from Alabama, are you?" he asked, turning to look at each of us.

"No," we said, again in unison.

"He had been driving already for a day and night," the boy began. "His plan was to drive all the way from Alabama to California without stopping. You are not from California, are you?" he asked and looked around the circle at our faces.

"No," we said, shaking our heads—in unison, of course.

"No way," I added, just to show a little variety.

"Well, he was on his way to El Paso, not too far from here, when he saw what looked like an old woman walking by the side of the road. It was three a.m., and he was feeling very sleepy. 'I'll give her a ride. She can keep me awake,' he said to himself.

"He slowed his car up beside her and rolled down the window.

"Do you need a ride?' he said.

"Need a ride,' the woman replied. She kept her shawl over her face.

"OK. I will be glad to take you. Where are you going?'

"'Where you going?' said the woman.

"'I'm going all the way to California. Let me help you in the car.' He left his car door open and headlights on. He walked around the car and opened the door for the old woman. She didn't move. She did not move away. She did not step in the car. She stood where she was, exactly where she was.

"The man was confused, then he thought, *Maybe she is too old to step into the car. Maybe I should help her.* So he lifted the woman and put her in the car. He made sure her dress and legs were inside before shutting the door. As he walked in front of his headlights the man had his first feeling that something was not right.

"He realized the woman had never really said anything to him. She had only repeated the last of everything he said. But the way she felt, that was the strangest thing of all. The man stood in his headlight beams in the middle of the highway and started talking loudly to himself.

"'When you pick up something, you know what it will feel like, even *before* you pick it up. A pencil feels like a pencil. You can pick it up with two fingers. A cat feels like a cat. It is light-weight and you can pick it up with both hands. A hurt child is heavier; you carry him close to your chest. You know what these things feel like *before* you pick them up. But the woman I just placed in my car, she didn't feel human!' He laughed and shook his head.

"'What am I saying?' He looked to the woman, hoping she had not heard him. She was slumped against the passenger door with her shawl pulled high over her head. 'I am so sleepy I am not thinking straight.' He slammed the car door and started the engine.

"When he turned to speak to the old woman, she seemed

peaceful and quiet, so he said nothing. He drove for twenty minutes without saying a word. Then he noticed the car was driving in a sputtering way, slowing to forty, even thirty-five miles an hour, then speeding up to seventy. Back and forth, slow to fast and back again.

"'What is happening?' he asked himself. Then he noticed that he was rocking, back and forth. His foot on the gas pedal was also rocking, causing the car to speed up and slow down in rhythm to the rocking. He laughed out loud and turned to the woman to tell her what was happening.

"She was no longer sitting quietly as before. The old woman was herself rocking back and forth. Soon she began a coughing sound, a heavy coughing from deep in her throat. He lifted his hand to hit her on the back, to keep the old woman from choking. He stopped himself and was glad he did, for she was not choking. She was clearing her throat to sing. She began a slow chant, an old Indian chant like he had never heard.

> Way hey hey ya
> Way hey hey ya,
> Way hey hey ya,
> Way hey hey ya.

"The sound was deep and scary. The man was too afraid to say a word. Then he heard another voice singing the song, a voice coming from behind him, a deeper voice.

> Way hey hey ya
> Way hey hey ya,
> Way hey hey ya,
> Way hey hey ya.

"*I left the car door open when I helped her in the car!* thought the man. *Maybe a friend of hers crawled in the back seat when I wasn't looking.* The sound grew louder and louder till it filled the car. He reached slowly behind himself, trying to watch the road at the same time. The singing was so close to him, but there was nobody there.

"Then he knew why. The sound, the chanting sound, was coming from his very own mouth. He was singing the song! He shook his head and looked to the old woman. She sang and rocked, back and forth.

Way hey hey ya
Way hey hey ya.

"Now the car was shaking, and when he looked at the speedometer, he was driving a hundred and five miles an hour. The chanting made his body fall asleep. His leg was dead, with no feeling. He couldn't lift it from the gas pedal.

"The man thought about kicking his sleeping leg with the other leg, kicking it from the gas pedal. 'But what if both legs fall on the brake? I could never survive a sudden stop at a hundred miles an hour,' he said aloud.

"Now the car was going a hundred and twenty. He tried to lift his arm from the steering wheel to touch the woman, to make her stop singing. His arm was asleep, too. He slowly pried his fingers from the steering wheel. With all of his willpower he lifted his arm. He tapped the woman.

"Suddenly, she fell silent. He pulled her shawl down to see her face. She had no skin. Where her hair and skin should have been, he saw animal fur. *Maybe she wore animal fur beneath her shawl because of the cold,* he thought.

"He reached to pull the animal fur away. He touched an ear on the fur. The ear twitched. *The fur is alive,* he thought. *It is part of her! What is this thing?*

"The man from Alabama never knew the answer, for his car slammed into a tree trunk at a hundred and twenty-five miles an hour.

"The next morning when the highway patrolman reached the scene of the accident, he opened the car door, but the driver wasn't there. Luckily, the man had been wearing his seat belt. He sat terrified and speechless a few feet from the tree. The front of his car was smashed like cardboard, and the steering wheel hung from the treetop.

"The patrolman said to himself, *I guess he was trying to save money on a motel. Looks like maybe a deer ran in front of him. Maybe he fell asleep at the wheel.*

"The patrolman called an ambulance. While he was waiting, a group of Navajos who lived nearby appeared. They heard what the patrolman said.

"'Wasn't no deer run across the road,' they said to each other. 'Wasn't anybody falling asleep at the wheel. Was Skinwalker! See the tracks,' they said, pointing to a set of tracks leading into the hills."

"Did you like the story?" the boy asked.

Some of us shook our heads, some of us nodded.

"Well," he continued, "like it or not, listen to the warning. When you are driving late at night in these west Texas hills, whatever you do, don't pick up any hitchhikers. Might not be a hitchhiker at all. Might be Skinwalker. You might not live to tell about it."

The boy turned to go.

"What is your name?" my father asked.

"Call me Nadie," said the boy.

"Nadie?" My father turned to us, hoping we might know the name. We lifted our shoulders as if to say, "We don't know," all in unison.

When my father turned to the boy, he was gone.

21

The Gypsy Drum

Her mother was irritated the first time she saw Tar's dark eye shadow and buzzcut short black hair. "Who cut your hair?" she asked at the supper table the first night of the *big change*. Tar was twelve and was hanging out with the middle school crowd.

"A friend," Tar answered, sneering her lip in a way she would do more and more over the coming weeks, till everyone who knew her came to expect it.

"Did she use a pocketknife?" asked Manny, her seven-year-old brother.

"No, you freaky little kid," she said.

"Tar, listen to what you're saying," her mother said.

"Why? No one else does," said Tar, and the match was on. From that day forward every meal, every family gathering, every shopping trip became a battleground between Tar and her mother. Tar especially hated those once-a-week trips to the grocery.

Mrs. Trane, Manny, and little sister Blue, barely eight years old, sat in the front seat. Tar leaned against the back door while baby Isaac snuggled in his car seat next to her.

"Can anybody tell me why I have to be here?"

"You are here to watch after your little brothers while I shop."

"I can do that at home."

"You could if I could trust you to stay home."

"Yeah, and stop having your goth boyfriends over when Mom's not home," said Manny. Tar planted a knuckle on the back of Manny's head.

"Owww!"

"Do you want me to pull this car over?"

"Pull-leeze do. I'd like to get out."

Her grades plummeted, childhood friends stopped calling and dropping by, and no more volleyball or soccer tryouts, not for Tar. She seemed determined to be happy in her misery, asking for nothing except for "everybody to please leave me alone," as she said one night before slamming her bedroom door.

Late November, her mother asked, "What would you like for Christmas, Tar?"

"Tats and rings, and I get to choose," replied Tar. "And same with the eye shadow. My choice," she added, ending that conversation. Christmas came and went and so did Tar's presents. One by one she took them from brightly colored boxes and twisted her lip. "Yeah. Like I'm really gonna wear this."

"Whatever," as she held high a red vinyl purse from an aunt.

By mid-January her presents had all made their way to the

trashcan on pickup day. Though all who knew her spoke of the change in Tar, the biggest change was yet to come. That change came with Presidents' Day, February 16.

School was out, and most downtown businesses closed for the parade around the town square. Marching bands from several nearby schools played John Philip Sousa and Francis Scott Key, gymnasts flipped, and Shriners clowned and funned their way through the cheering crowd. Hundreds of tents of every color were spread over the grounds of the county courthouse. The tents held tables of pottery, jewelry, and crafts of other kinds.

"The parade is something we can do as a family," Mrs. Trane said that morning. Tar sneered. But to her surprise, she did enjoy the afternoon. Her mother and her friends brought lawn chairs and found a shaded spot to visit and watch the floats, and Tar was able to slip away for a few hours.

"Take Blue with you!" her mother called over the noise of yet another version of "Seventy-Six Trombones." Tar didn't mind, for little sister Blue was gradually taking after her, starting with the eye shadow, though she hid it from her mother.

The sisters watched part of the parade from the sidewalk, then eased toward the alley around the corner. Tar looked for her friends but couldn't find them in the crowd. As she stepped from the curb, she spotted a small tent in the alley, little more than an awning stretched between two buildings. Made of heavy blue cloth, the tent stood in the shadows and was dark and uninviting.

A single flap served as an entrance. Painted on the blue flap was a golden five-pointed star, tilted in such a way that Tar was drawn to it. Peering inside, Tar saw a table covered with candles and bowls of handmade pottery.

In a corner she saw a rack of long scarves, scarves tie-dyed with streaks of purple and red. Tar stepped to the scarves and ran her fingers across the smooth silk cloth. Before her eyes adjusted to the darkness, something floated over her shoulders.

"This should be more to your liking," a voice whispered in her ear. Tar turned to see a gypsy woman with three golden rings, one through a nostril and two on her top lip. Her hair was black, naturally black, and a dark blue scarf cast a shadow over her face.

"My name is Blythe," the woman said. "What is yours?"

"Tar, and this is my sister Blue."

"Good names for bad girls," said the gypsy. "Do you like your scarf?" Tar lowered her eyes to see a black silk scarf draped over her shoulders.

"Yes," she said. "I like it very much."

"Do you have money?"

"Yes," said Tar, reaching for her pocket. "How much is the scarf?"

"Oh," laughed the gypsy, "the scarf is not for money, no. The scarf is for you. But I have some shadow for your eyes you will like, nice and thick powder." She opened her palm, and on it sat a short fat jar. "Five dollars."

"I want it," said Tar, and gave her the money.

At that moment a tapping sound began, a tapping of wood on tin. The gypsy stepped aside. Behind her sat a strange girl in layers of dark clothing. Her eyes were downcast and she was playing a drum. As Tar and Blue watched, the top of the drum opened and a tiny twirling figure of a man emerged, spinning round and round as the tapping continued. Neither could later say how long the dancing man spun. When he finally returned to the drum and the tin top covered him over, Tar looked at Blue.

"We want the drum," she said.

"You want the drum?" said the gypsy, laughing. "Well, you cannot have the drum. Not for money."

"We want the drum," repeated Tar.

"Well, if you want the drum, you must be bad. Come see me tomorrow and tell me how bad you've been," the gypsy said, and soon the sisters found themselves on the sidewalk.

That evening after supper Mrs. Trane said, "I am exhausted. Can you girls wash and dry the dishes and get your brother to bed? I will tend to the baby."

As soon as their mother closed the door to her room, Tar and Blue filled the sink with soapy water and began scrubbing dishes. Tar lifted a large platter of white and sky-blue china. It was her mother's finest dish, a gift from her own mother. Tar held it overhead and turned it over, then dropped it to the floor.

The thin glass shattered. The girls looked at each other and waited. Nothing happened. Nobody heard, so they swept the broken glass in the folds of a magazine and buried the shards in the backyard flower bed.

Sunday morning the girls returned to the gypsy tent in the alley. The flap was closed. They stood staring for only a moment, then came the tapping, the tinny tapping of the drum. The gypsy flung open the flap, and the girls entered just as the man returned to the drum and the top closed over him.

"Were you bad?" the gypsy asked.

"Oh, yes," said Tar. "We were bad. Our mother doesn't even know how bad we were. We broke her favorite dish, a china platter from her family. We broke it and buried it in the flower bed."

The gypsy laughed and flung back her head. "You broke your mother's dish," she said, in a mocking tone. "You broke a dish! That is not bad. You cannot have the drum, and I am leaving."

"Where are you going?" asked Tar.

"To the campgrounds by the river," said the gypsy.

Once again the sisters found themselves on the sidewalk. On the way home Tar noticed, in the reflection of a window, something Blue had seen since morning. Tar's eyeshadow was blacker than ever, and thick as calloused skin.

"Where have you girls been?" shouted their mother when they entered the house.

"Nowhere," said Tar. Blue hid behind her sister.

"I found my mother's china dish in the flower bed—what was left of it. Any idea how it got there?"

Blue started to speak, but Tar squeezed her arm, saying, "Are you accusing us of something?"

"Yes," her mother said. "I am accusing you girls of being up to something, some dark and secret something. Whatever you think you can do, you need to remember this. When you do bad things, bad things happen to you."

Tar looked past her mother as if she wasn't there.

"I have plans today and I need you to keep your brothers. Make sandwiches for lunch," her mother said, and drove away.

An hour later Tar said, "Are you ready, Blue?" Blue nodded and followed her sister out the door. "Let's see a movie. Who's to stop us? But first, let's find some stones."

The sisters found six heavy stones, too heavy for pockets but not too heavy to throw. Tar threw first. Her stone smashed the kitchen window.

The girls left behind six broken windows and two terrified brothers, and fifteen minutes later were settled into their seats at the local cinema, enjoying their first taste of hot buttered popcorn.

After the movie Tar and Blue took the path to the river. The sun was going and the day turned dark. The gypsy's tent was attached to the side of her van, and a lantern shone from inside. As they neared the tent the girl began to play. The tiny drum sent out a sound so loud it rattled the leaves of nearby trees.

"Were you bad?" asked the gypsy as the sisters stood before her.

"Very, very bad," said Tar. "We left our brothers alone at home and broke six windows before going."

"Well," said the gypsy, "for little girls like you, that is bad. But not bad enough. Go home."

Tar and Blue stood staring at the river.

When they returned home their mother was waiting for them in the living room. "Your brothers saw you break the windows," she said. "I don't know what is going on, but you two must change. I mean it. When you do bad things, bad things happen to you. You've got to stop it!"

"Or what?" said Tar.

"Or this. If you do not return to the girls you were, I will no longer be your mother. Your new mother will have one glass eye and wooden hands."

"What are you saying?" asked Tar, sneering as never before.

"Do not doubt me," said her mother.

"You never touch us anyway," said Blue. "What difference would wooden hands make?"

The next morning Mother took Manny and the baby with her.

"We are really close now. Don't you feel it?" said Tar.

Blue nodded and stuck her finger in the jar of eye shadow, as if it were pudding and she a starving orphan. She smeared the paste around her eyes and pinched her bottom lip.

"Let's do the laundry," said Tar. "Mother would like that."

Blue did not move.

"Tar?"

"What?"

"Do you remember what Mother said?" Blue asked. "When you do bad things, bad things happen to you."

Tar stared at her little sister for a long moment. "Your eye shadow looks great," she finally said, pinching Blue's cheek and turning to the task.

Tar gathered towels and skirts and several of her mother's blouses and piled them all in the bathtub. She took bleach from the washing room and poured the gallon bottle over the pile.

"So much for laundry," she said. "What other chores need doing? Maybe the wallpaper?"

Blue brought knives from the kitchen and the sisters hacked and sliced and cut away till not a room was left undone. Wallpaper hung in tatters.

The rest you can imagine.

The gypsy waited. The girl played the drum. The sisters entered the tent.

"We want the drum," said Tar.

"Then tell me of your day, how bad you were," the gypsy said.

"We were so bad," said Tar. "We know the drum is ours." She told the gypsy everything.

The gypsy nodded slowly.

"Yes," she finally said. "You girls were bad, worse than ever I thought you could be. But you can't have the drum. The drum is mine and you can never have it."

So once again the girls stood staring at the river.

When they returned home the house was empty and cold. Tar and Blue spent the remainder of the day in their room. Dark came, and they huddled together beneath a quilt in a corner.

The wind slipped quietly through the broken windows and chilled the sisters.

Blue clung to Tar and cried. "When you do bad things, bad things happen to you," she said, over and over, so softly till the words became a whisper of cold air.

The moon rose high, casting a pale glow against the bedroom door. Tar and her little sister Blue heard heavy footsteps scraping down the hall. A wrenching, scratching sound sent shivers through their skin; the sound of nails dragged across the wooden walls. The doorknob slowly turned and the door opened. A dark shadow stood where once the moon had glowed. A strange face leaned through the crack in the doorway.

One red glass eyeball peered at the sisters.

"I am your new mother," came a crackling voice, and two wooden hands reached for the girls.

The Woman with Cat's Eyes

My mother loved that little dwarf. Everybody did. He had the cutest little pointed beard and hat and his boots came above his knees, like in old storybooks. Why did Miss Mandrake have to take the dwarf? I would never have thrown her eyeballs in the fire if she hadn't taken the dwarf.

OK, now that I have aroused your interest, hopefully, with what Miss Turner, my fourth-grade teacher, calls "A grabber beginning," we can backtrack and begin the story, though I always prefer more blood in the introduction. Something like,

"When Miss Mandrake returned home from her late-night

prowling and heard her eyeballs sizzling and popping in the fireplace, she grabbed what she thought was the fireplace poker, but it was a butcher knife. She accidentally sliced off her thumb. It went rolling under her coffee table, spreading a dark red spot on her sky-blue Navajo rug . . . *Yeah! So maybe she bites her thumb to stop the bleeding and blood flows from her empty eye sockets! Now we're getting somewhere!*

OK, one of the toughest things about writing is to control the crazy urges and just tell the story. So . . .

Since I get home from school earlier than my mother gets home from work, I was the first to notice that the dwarf was missing from the flower bed. Only a two-inch imprint in the soil remained. My dad had given it to her two years ago for graduation from that six-week eat-all-you-want-and-lose-weight yoga class at the Tai Chi Warrior Studio, so it was very special to her. I even planted a dozen yellow marigolds around the dwarf's boots.

When I saw the dwarf was missing, I knew trouble was coming. That night was *Monday Night Football,* and the Cowboys were playing the Indians, as my dad always called them. Actually, they are the Washington Redskins, but Dad says that's not very respectful. I never really know if he's kidding or not.

But whoever the Cowboys were playing, we had a houseful of people, all there because my mom makes the best nachos in the universe and we have a wall-length high-definition television set. "Better than being at the game!" says loud old Mr. Beeson, every Monday night.

I first heard Mom mention the dwarf after she put the first

platter of nachos in the microwave, a few minutes before kick-off.

"Did you move Grumpy from the flower bed?" she asked my dad. When my dad gave her one of his *What are you talking about?* looks, she said, "Grumpy. You know, the dwarf."

"Nope," he said. "Me and Grumpy don't hang out that much anymore. Why do you ask?"

"Well, somebody moved him. Duke," she turned to me, "you didn't move Grumpy, did you? Or accidentally break him?"

"No way, Mom. When I got home from school, he was already gone." She pursed her lips and sprinkled grated cheese on another platter of killer nachos.

"What's missing?" asked Mrs. Tottingham, stepping from the living room and carrying a bag of ice to the sink.

"My dwarf," said Mom.

"Grumpy?"

"Grumpy's missing?" asked Mrs. Wallerbee, coming in through the back door with a case of Dr. Pepper over her shoulder. My best friend Jason followed her, dragging a had-to-be forty-pound bag of chips.

"I noticed that when I first drove up," said Mrs. Toliver, refrigerating her Tupperware container of deviled eggs. *I hate those rubbery, squirmy things!*

"Well, your front yard just won't be the same without old Grumpy!" said Mr. Wallerbee, easing a case of root beer to the table and scooting out of the kitchen as fast as he could. "No more Yard of the Month for you," he said in passing.

So the topic of kitchen discussion was set for the evening. *Who took Grumpy?* At least that was the opening topic, but by the end of the first quarter, ten women were huddled around the table talking about things missing from their yards. A garden hoe from the Tottinghams, a rope swing from the Tolivers, even a small barbeque grill from the Wallerbees. But the tone was light and gossipy, and whenever somebody scored, everyone turned their attention to the game.

Till Mrs. Belvedere spoke. She was a widow, a sweet seventy-five-year-old retired music teacher. She only came to our Monday night events to keep from being alone.

"Somebody came into my house in the middle of the night last week and stole my violin," she said. She spoke softly, but her tone was stern and serious. A hush fell over the kitchen and she continued.

"My violin instructor from Hartford College presented it to me fifty-three years ago. I was his best student ever, he told me, and since he was retiring, he wanted me to have it. Someone came in through the washing room window. I saw dirty footprints on the tile floor. They stole my violin from the ebony wood table in my music room."

No one spoke for a long moment.

"Did you call the police?" asked Mrs. Toliver.

"Yes, I drove to the police station to report the theft. Two days later, when they finally came to my house, I had already mopped the mud from the floor. They think I am so old I just misplaced the violin."

The Cowboys won in overtime; that was the big news from the living room. But the missing items from the neighborhood—that was news that wouldn't go away. A thief in Sherwood Forest!

Jason and I heard everything, scooting from the kitchen to the ballgame and back again. When his parents were leaving, he motioned for me to follow him to the curb. "I think I know who's been taking that stuff," he said. "You know the funny-acting woman who moved in around the corner? She goes out every night. I see her leaving from my bedroom window, but then she just kinda disappears."

"I've never even seen her," I said.

"Almost nobody has. She only comes out at night."

"Get in the car, Jason," his mother called. "You've got school tomorrow."

"I'll see you later," he whispered. "Make sure you have good batteries in your flashlight."

Less than an hour later I lay on my back trying to imagine what a lady who broke into houses and stole things from people's yards in the middle of the night would look like. Skinny and evil, I thought, with a curled upper lip and scraggly hair pulled back in a bun. I laughed out loud, realizing I was picturing Miss Burnwell, our substitute teacher from last year. Her name was actually Miss Burnell, but Burnwell seemed to fit her better, once we realized her witchy ways.

What would a witch look like today? Would she dress in all black like a goth? Would one eye shift from side to side? Would she talk in a hissing whisper? Would her teeth grow into pointy fangs, like in those vampire books? I fell asleep with these thoughts, never a good way to enter dreamland, and soon saw a dark mist rising from around my bed and a thin hand with sharp nails reaching for me. That's when Jason woke me up.

"It's time." That's all he said. Jason never wasted words. I found my flashlight and crawled out my bedroom window.

"She hasn't left yet. It's still early." He was walking fast, and I had to hustle to catch up with him. We turned the corner and moved in the direction of Jason's street. We stopped at a red brick house facing his and settled in a clump of shiny-leafed shrubs on the side of the house.

We had a good view of the front yard of Miss Mandrake, our

newest neighbor. Five minutes later the door eased open and she stepped into the shadows of her entryway, hidden from the street by a trellis of trumpet vines. She was a tall, thin woman, and her neck stretched from her shoulders like a swan's. She wore a dark blue dress with sleeves that hung to her wrists and a hood that covered her face.

In the time it took her to slip from behind the trellis and lift her arms to the moonless sky, Miss Mandrake was gone. She didn't race away with the speed of a gazelle, nor did she flap her arms and fly. She simply disappeared, so suddenly that if Jason had not prepared me for such an occurrence, I would have thought I imagined it all.

"See," he said. "Whatever she is, she's not one of us."

No words came to me, so I stood up slowly and nodded. My mouth hung open and my eyes bugged out. "I want some hot chocolate," I said. "You think your mom would make us some hot chocolate?"

I knew it sounded dumb, but I didn't care. I did not want to do whatever Jason was planning. I did not want to go wherever he was leading us. I wanted hot chocolate.

"Mom is asleep and we're out of hot chocolate," he said. "But it *is* one thirty in the morning, and we *are* about to enter the house of a witch who lives across the street from me. That will have to be enough for tonight."

I snapped out of my stupor and held up my flashlight.

"Are you sure she's gone?" I asked.

"I guess we can't be sure of anything," he said, "but I don't think she went back in the house." He nodded in the direction of the backyard gate. We lifted the latch, but the gate refused to budge.

"Nailed shut from the inside," Jason said, and before I could reply he had scaled the fence. "Toss me the flashlight and come on."

I flung the light and leapt to reach the splintering boards of the gate. I scrambled over the top, but my right hand slipped and I caught an inch-long sliver of pine under a fingernail before falling rump-first on the pebbles below. "Oww!"

"Shhhh! In case you don't know, we're not in Kansas anymore," Jason reminded me.

Miss Mandrake's backyard was unlike anything I had ever seen in the world of the sane. Three tall elm trees shaded the patio, just as they did in every yard in Sherwood Forest. But unlike any other backyard in our neighborhood, from every tree hung twirling shapes of wood, bones, and feathers. Limbs sagged with the weight of triangles made of iron, one painted blue with bright yellow stars, another dark green with tiny perforations.

Light danced through the holes and bounced from the moon to the metal to the eye, giving the entire yard the feeling of vibrating air. The very ground seemed to throb beneath our feet. As if to balance the sharp edges of the math-born shapes, animal skins, soft and thick with fur, dangled from smaller branches like living laundry on a witch's wash line.

We stood without speaking for ten minutes. The wind and passing clouds added to the colorful spectacle.

A low hissing sound returned us to the world of the living. From a limb above our heads came the soft moan of a beast, and when Jason swung his flashlight to the sound, I knew instantly what was about to happen. The beast leapt from the tree onto my back and began clawing my neck and throat. I lifted my arms to protect myself, but the thing was quick and sank its claws deep in the skin behind my ears.

I was finally able to reach over my head and fling the howling creature to the ground. It landed on four feet and seemed ready to pounce again, when I realized it was a large house cat, a black cat with one alarming feature.

The cat had no eyeballs. Two empty sockets glared up at me, glowing green eye sockets. The cat dashed to the house and entered through a flap at the bottom of the door.

"Are you sure you don't have any hot chocolate?" I asked, trying with a joke to regain my foothold on reality.

"I'm glad you can't see yourself," replied Jason.

I wiped what felt like sweat from my eyes, then noticed my shirt was soaked in blood. I felt painful scratches on my cheeks, neck, and shoulders. "That was one strong cat," I said.

"I think we better go home now," said Jason. I knew I must look a bloody mess. Jason was never the cautious one. We were moving to the gate when he shined the flashlight through Miss Mandrake's kitchen window.

"Stop!" I yelled. "There it is!" Grumpy, my mother's dwarf, was sitting on the kitchen table. "I'm not leaving it here another night."

"Duke, we need to leave. We've made a lot of noise."

"Jason, that's my mom's dwarf!" I tried the back door and, to our surprise, it opened.

"I don't like what we're doing," Jason said, as we entered the witch's house. He turned off the light as I hurried to the dwarf and placed it carefully under my right arm.

"Duke, you've got to see this!" Jason called from the living room. I set the dwarf on the table and found Jason standing beside a monstrous stone fireplace. His face appeared red in the

soft glow of dying embers. His eyes were larger than life, and I
followed his pointing finger to a small antique table.

Two human eyeballs stared back at us. They sat a few inches
apart and appeared shiny and wet, as if they had only recently
been removed. "Those don't belong to any cat," he said. As if in
reply, the sound of footsteps came from the front porch.

"She's come back," I whispered.

Miss Mandrake stood behind the trellis. We watched through
a curtained window as she lifted her fingers to her eyes and removed two green cat's eyes from her sockets. We were terrified
and knew that even the slightest movement would send her after
us. She entered the front door and slowly felt her way toward
the table, moving to her eyes.

We had the same thought. I reached Miss Mandrake's eyeballs first and hurled them into the fire.

"Run!" we both hollered, and while she knocked over the
table in her haste to grab her eyeballs, we scurried past her and
in a few minutes were crawling in Jason's window.

As we sat panting on his bedroom floor, leaning against the
wall, I imagined a popping sound, two popping sounds, and in
my mind's eye saw a pair of eyeballs shrink and shrivel in Miss
Mandrake's fireplace. We fell asleep without moving.

"What are you two doing?" his mother asked the next morning. "Where have you been?"

I told her everything. While we cleaned up and dressed for
school, she made phone calls. At 10:00 a.m. the police arrived
at Miss Mandrake's house. She answered the door after five
minutes of loud knocking and refused to allow them to enter.
She wore, according to Jason's mother, a pair of dark sun-
glasses.

"I will come down to the station later and file charges against two boys who broke into my house last night," she said, then closed the door.

Of course, she never appeared at the police station. The following day, Wednesday, when she did not answer her door, the police shouldered it open and found her gone. She took only a small amount of clothing, "by the looks of things," said one officer to a gathering throng of Sherwood Forest residents.

Miss Mandrake was apparently renting the house. When the landlord heard of her leaving without paying the month's rent, he had a garage sale of her belongings. Curious neighbors filled the front yard one bright and sunny Saturday. People from outside Sherwood Forest did most of the buying. Mr. Beeson summed our feelings up best.

"I wouldn't have anything belonging to that strange woman in my house!" he said.

Jason and I wandered among the folding tables, helping Mrs. Belvedere locate her violin, the Wallerbees their grill. Just after noon Jason lifted a pile of towels from a cardboard box and gestured for me to see what he'd found. He pointed, and I looked.

"Just when you thought it was safe to go back in the water," I muttered, a reference to an old movie called *Jaws*. Sitting in the bottom of the box was a cement cat, *her* cat, with no eyeballs. The two sockets still shone with a faint glow.

Jason grabbed the cat and hurried to the landlord.

"How much?" he asked.

"Oh, let's say a dollar and a quarter." We pooled our coins and came up a dime short.

"No problem," replied the balding landlord, his mind fixed on the golf round he was missing. Jason turned to the old rock quarry and began to run. I knew his intentions. When he reached the edge of the quarry, he waited for me.

"Good-bye to the first real danger we've ever known," he said, and flung the cement cat to the boulders below. We didn't stay to watch the cat shatter into a heap of dust and tiny rocks.

Maybe that was for the best, for the cat did not shatter against the boulders. In fact, the cat never reached the boulders. Instead, it came to life halfway into its fall and clung to a thick tree root sticking through the quarry wall. It then flipped around the root and climbed to the top.

By the time the two boys were sipping their hot chocolate, the cat with no eyeballs crouched on the lap of blind Miss Mandrake, curling and purring as the witch planned her next move.

The Monkey's Paw

Near the turn of the last century, a man, his wife, and their son George moved to a small town in deep East Texas. The old man was retired from a long career as a merchant, filling orders at a hardware store in Dallas. His wife was crippled from the kick of a mule years ago. Though every step she took sent a sharp pain coursing through her hip, she somehow managed to cook and clean and struggle through the day.

George was young and strong, with broad shoulders and long brown hair curling around his collar. His six brothers and sisters had married and moved away while George was still in his teens, and George accepted the responsibility of caring for his aging parents. He worked in the local sawmill, running thick pine trunks through the buzz saw. The job was dangerous and required strength, a steady hand, and sharp eyesight.

George walked to work every morning and returned home just after sundown, exhausted and covered with sawdust. Every evening he pleaded with his father.

"Dad, please listen to me. I can find work in the city. I will send you enough money to live on, more money than I could ever earn at the mill."

"Look at your mother," his father said. "She needs you here, and I am too old to support us. I desperately need your help. You are the only family left to us. We need much more than money."

George turned away and sank into a deep sadness.

"Son," his father said. "A miracle is coming. I feel it. We are in the midst of a miracle. Wait and see."

One night over a supper of white beans and ham, the three sat listening to the hissing sound of logs catching fire. The wind howled in the piney woods and branches struck the sagging wallboards of the house. After tending to the dishes, the old woman sat by the fireplace sipping her coffee while the old man paced the room.

"I guess the Sergeant Major won't be coming over tonight," the father said. Lightning struck a tree nearby and thunder shook the fragile wooden house.

"Your friend has never missed a Friday for the past five years," she said. "He will come. Wait and see." Soon, they were startled by a knock at the door. When the father answered the knock, the Sergeant Major stood at the door, drenched and shivering.

"Let me in, please. I am chilled to the bone." The two older people exchanged glances, for the Sergeant Major never spoke to them this way. The old man stepped aside, and his distinguished friend settled into a cane back rocking chair by the fire. The father took his friend's coat, and the four sat silently for almost half an hour.

"The road was slick with sleet. I fell several times on the walk. I feel very lucky to be here," the Sergeant Major said.

"We are so glad you came. We were worried about you," said the mother.

"Did you bring your playing cards?" asked the old man.

"I have my cards but have no desire to play," said the Sergeant Major. "I am afraid my strength is gone. I may need to stay the night, if you have a place for me."

"Of course. You should not be walking in this freezing rain. The wind is enough to blow a stronger man than you to the ground," said the father.

The old friends sat listening to the icy rain for the better part of an hour. Finally, the Sergeant Major said, "I guess we should play a few hands. If nothing else, it will take our minds off the weather."

As he reached in his vest pocket for his playing cards, a red handkerchief fell to the floor, and from it rolled a small dark object.

"What in the world is that?" asked the old man.

"Nothing. Never mind. This is not for your eyes!" shouted the Sergeant Major, and turned his gaze to the fire. The silence that followed was strange and unfriendly. Young George gave words to the question hovering in the air.

"What was that thing?" he asked. "It looked like the hand of a small human, but I've never seen a hairy hand like that."

"Only a trinket I picked up on my last trip to India," said the Sergeant Major. "Nothing about this concerns you."

"Then why did you bring it?" asked George.

"Why are you hiding it?" asked Father.

The Sergeant Major took a long, deep sigh before replying. "If you must know, I have carried this handkerchief with me for twenty years, long and tragic years. I am ready to be rid of it."

"What is in the handkerchief?" asked George. The Sergeant Major lifted his gaze to the young man, as if his words carried a heavy burden.

"It is called a monkey's paw," he said. "This monkey's paw will give the owner three wishes."

"Three wishes!" shouted George. "You mean I might be finished with the sawmill?"

"Yes," said the Sergeant Major. "If that be your desire. But I must warn you, nothing but evil ever comes from the monkey's paw."

"Nothing but evil?" shouted George.

"You will not talk to our guest this way," his father said.

"Let him have his say," said the mother. "He deserves at least to speak, with all he does to support us."

Ignoring them, George approached the Sergeant Major. "Nothing but evil?" he repeated. His voice was barely a whisper, but his eyes grew large and his whole body began to shake. He rolled his left sleeve to his elbow and spread his fingers apart, six inches from the Sergeant Major's face. "Would you like to see evil? I will show you evil."

The Sergeant Major stared at the hand that was missing its two middle fingers. "There is no evil on earth like the evil that lives in the sawmill," said George.

"How does it work?" asked the old man.

"If you must know, place the monkey's paw in your palm. Hold it up and make your wish. If your hand begins to quiver

48

and shake, you can be sure the wish will be granted."

"Great! I want it," said George. "Maybe just for a month."

"No," said the Sergeant Major, "let us do what should have been done years ago." He tossed the monkey's paw into the fire. The tiny hand popped and smoked but could not, or would not, burn. The old man dragged it from the fireplace, shaking burning ashes from his arm.

"Give it to me!" cried the Sergeant Major, but the old man refused, clutching it behind his back.

"I beg of you, throw it away!" said the Sergeant Major.

"No!" the old man and George called out in unison.

The Sergeant Major stepped away from them. He looked through the window. He saw that the sleet had ceased and lightning no longer cut the dark night air. Without another word, he slipped on his jacket and left, slamming the door behind him. The family stood frozen in surprise.

The old man, his wife, and young George gathered by the fire.

"Three wishes?" said the old man.

"Three wishes," repeated the old woman.

"Is this the miracle you spoke of? Can I now leave the sawmill?" asked George.

"Could be," said the father. "But I think we should ask for something smaller to begin with, to test what sort of evil comes with the wish."

"How about maybe two hundred dollars?" suggested the woman. The old man nodded and held the paw above his head.

"We wish for two hundred dollars!" he shouted. The paw began to shift and shake in his open palm, then fell to the floor.

The day had been stressful for the family, and soon everyone crept quietly to their beds and fell asleep. The next morning

49

George arose and prepared his lunch. After a simple breakfast of fatback and biscuits, he left for his day at the mill. No one said a word about the Sergeant Major, the wish, or the monkey's paw.

An hour before noon, a mild knock sounded at the door. A young man about George's age stood holding his hat, with downcast eyes. He was well dressed and carried an envelope.

"I have some very bad news for you," he said. "This morning, when the saw blades were turned to their top speed, for some reason, some unexplainable reason, George left his station at the back of the saw and moved to the blade. Everyone tried to stop him but could not. He was cut to pieces."

He waited for a response, but the old man and woman only clung to each other without speaking.

"Now, this was an accident. The mill takes no responsibility. But we took up a collection to help with burial expenses." He dropped an envelope on the table and left. The father followed him to the mill and insisted on seeing George's body, cut and sliced by the large mill saw.

The funeral was the following day, and a large number of mill employees attended. That night, the old man and his wife sat alone for the first time in half a century. Several times the old woman cried out, "He was my son! My son is gone! All because of the monkey's paw. I want my boy back! We can use the paw to bring him back."

Finally the old man gave in. He held the paw high and said, "Our son is gone. Please bring him back to us!"

The paw shook and quivered and fell to the floor. The couple stayed awake late, sharing memories of George, from the day of his birth till his final night on earth.

Just after midnight they heard something approaching the

house—the sound of dragging feet. Closer and closer came the sound. After having trouble with thieves and robbers, the old man had placed four locks on the door. One by one the woman unlocked them, and readied herself to open the door.

"Stop!" said the old man. "You do not want to see what I saw."

"My boy," she said. "I want my boy back!" Off came the fourth lock. The old man grabbed the paw and lifted it high, shouting.

"Please send our son back to the world of the dead," he said, "back to his grave, where he must remain!"

The old woman looked through the door and into the yard. She saw nothing, or almost nothing. The two gates swung back and forth, but whatever had passed through them was gone. They returned to their chairs by the fire and did not sleep till morning.

In olden times, many people carried a rabbit's foot for good luck. When rummaging through old boxes in the attic, if you happen to find among family belongings a large paw, a hairy paw, a monkey's paw, throw it away! You never know what will happen when you cast your fate to the monkey's paw!

Screaming Banshee Cattle of the Night Swamp

Right, *Dad. I'm really gonna believe that. The screaming banshee cattle of the night swamp.*

Jacob only *thought* these words. He had too much respect for his dad to actually say them.

Since the divorce, Jacob did his best to survive these twice-a-month late-night car trips from Orange to Pasadena. He spent every other weekend with his dad, a cool and funny but kind of crazy dad, a man who told the same dumb jokes and who never, like NEVER, arrived anywhere on time.

Jacob remembered sitting outside the lawyer's office and hearing the lawyer say, "Mister Carnes, do you fully understand what you are agreeing to do? Your son can visit you every other

weekend, but only if you return him to his mother's home by six o'clock Sunday evening."

Jacob didn't hear his father's response. He didn't have to. He knew his dad would lift his shoulders to his ears, open his palms, and say something like, "Duh!" Just because he was signing an important legal document in the downtown Houston office of a law firm, this was no reason for his dad to be serious, not *his* dad. "Duh?" Jacob had to smile at the thought of the look on the lawyer's face.

For the first two months his dad actually tried to get him home on time. Seven thirty. Eight fifteen. But now, six months into the agreement, it was more like nine thirty. A little after ten. With his dad making up stories to make everything all right.

Screaming banshee cattle of the night swamp, Jacob thought. As they drove over the bridge east of Beaumont, Jacob's dad pointed to a group of cattle grazing on the edge of a bayou.

"See," he said. "The cows with their legs in the water. That's them. They only leave the boggy depths when the clouds cover the moon and no one can see them. They only pretend to graze like other cattle, but they don't eat grass. Human flesh, that's all they eat. Once they step out of the water, their teeth grow long and sharp and their nostrils flare. They circle their victim, so quiet they appear like any other cattle, moving from one clump of grass to another."

Jacob sat up and his father smiled, seeing he had his son's attention.

"But they move with a purpose," he continued, "and when they have closed all avenues of escape, they pounce, devouring the unlucky one. When their bellies are filled, they creep back to the mud and slime to blend in with the rest of the herd. They wash their bloody tongues with swampwater till the morning comes and only the tattered flesh and bones remain of their latest victim. Yes, the latest victim of the screaming banshee cattle of the night swamp."

"Why do they call them *screaming* cattle?" asked Jacob.

"Oh, I almost forgot to tell you. They scream when they pounce, a piercing scream, more like a panther than a moocow."

"Oh. Okay, Dad, now it all makes sense. Thanks for clearing that up for me," said Jacob.

"Anytime, kid. That's what fathers are for."

Jacob pulled his jacket around him and leaned against the door of his dad's old pickup truck. The air conditioner didn't work. *Cool's better with the windows rolled down anyway,* his dad always said, and a two-foot-long crack snaked across the windshield. *From a sniper's bullet,* claimed his dad.

None of this bothered Jacob. At least the CD player worked, and when he wasn't telling stories his dad always played loud rock music, "Smoke on the Water," "Iron Man," even old Led Zeppelin songs.

> In the days of my youth
> I was told what it means to be a man.

That seemed to be a favorite. But tonight was different. No rock music blared from the door speakers. His dad fell silent while Jacob slept, easing into a dreamy world of murky swamps and flesh-eating cattle.

The door slammed and Jacob jumped, banging his head against the window glass. His dad had pulled into the parking lot of a roadside restaurant. The green wooden building sagged beneath the weight of cypress limbs and curly gray moss. Neon lights blinked off and on from the roof.

SAMSON'S CRAWDAD DINER

"I'll be right back. I'm gonna grab some burgers and fries," his dad said, disappearing into the diner. Jacob tried closing his eyes and going back to sleep, but something about the surroundings made him uneasy. He tugged at his cheek, a habit he had developed in recent months, and pulled his knees to his chest.

The diner sat fifty yards off the highway, down a dirt road full of chuckholes, and a rust-covered old Chevy seemed to be the only other car in the lot. A side building with a private door was attached to the diner; a dog dish filled with rainwater sat on the rubber welcome mat. *Somebody lives here,* thought Jacob. *Probably the owner.*

The wind whistled and Jacob leaned to see a thin sliver of moon, darting and ducking behind fast-moving clouds. He watched as a mountainous thunderhead rose over the moon and darkened everything—the sky, the diner, the parking lot, even the truck's interior. Jacob shivered, as much from the feeling brought on by the clouds as from the chilling air. Fat raindrops splattered on the windshield and Jacob felt trapped in a world of unseen danger. A crack of lightning cut the power, and now, for the first time since he was a young child, Jacob was afraid for his life.

With a sputtering uncertainty, the lights returned. Through the window of the diner Jacob saw his dad, sitting on a counter stool. He was cracking jokes with the cook, no doubt about the power outage. Jacob blinked hard and his chest heaved. In the diner, life appeared normal. *As normal as life ever is around my dad,* he thought, then felt a twinge of guilt at that disrespectful notion.

At first the girl's screams were little more than curious squeals, muffled by the wind. Jacob rolled the window down, shielding his face from the rain with his palms. He pushed open the door, but the wind was so strong it slammed the door shut, knocking him to the floorboard. The vinyl seat was soon wet and slick with rainwater. He flipped up the door handle, leaned shoulder-first, and lunged hard. The door gave way and he fell to the gravel.

Her screams were now so loud Jacob could not believe only he heard them. He considered dashing into the restaurant and calling to his dad. *But what if the screams are nothing?* he thought. *What if none of this is real?*

"Help me!" The call came from behind the building. Jacob righted himself and ran to the voice. He splashed through a checkerboard of mud puddles, slipped and landed hard on his back, and looked up just in time to dodge a heavy tree limb crashing six inches from his face. His eyes grew large as he stared at the size of the limb and realized how close he had come to waking up in the hospital.

In the next instant, Jacob wished he were in the hospital. A long piercing scream, high-pitched and murderous, joined the wind's howling. His first thought was to run, as fast and far away from this remote and fearful place as possible. Instead, he ran behind the building.

Twenty feet from the water's edge he saw the girl, not more than ten years old, he guessed. Her right arm stretched awkwardly behind her and her face writhed in pain. Her light hair flung about her shoulders. When she saw Jacob, she reached out for him, yanking her arm free and ripping her coat sleeve, but only for an instant.

Jacob halted his run by gripping a tree trunk. The girl was sliding away from him, crying and striving to free herself, but the teeth of the creature, a large cow, a simple jersey cow, a friendly black-and-white milk-giving cow, held tight to the girl's arm and was dragging her to the swamp, where six other cattle waited, their mouths wide open and screaming loud enough to send moss hurling from the trees and into the dark swampwaters below. Jacob released his hold on the tree and slid down the embankment.

Without knowing how, he managed to steady himself as he reached the girl. He gripped her outstretched hand and tugged hard. She cried again, and blood spurted from her forearm. The remaining cattle moved now east and west, drawing a circle around the two. Jacob knew that in only moments that shivering sound would slice the air and all seven of the screaming banshee cattle of the night swamp would pounce upon them, gnawing and grinding and tearing away at their evening meal of flesh, human flesh. *His* flesh, and that of the girl.

"Dad!" he called out. "Dad! Please come! Please help us!"

"Jacob!" came the response. He dared not take his eyes off the girl, but the look on her face told him his father was joining the fight.

"Oh no, not them!" The voice was one Jacob had never heard, a deep voice in an unfamiliar accent. He turned to look. His father was followed by the cook, an enormous man with bulging biceps and a chest as wide as a cypress stump. The cook picked up the fallen tree branch and began swinging at the cow. The creature bellowed and bawled and released the girl to go for the cook.

Jacob's father took his son under one arm, the girl under the other, and they struggled up the muddy slope while the cattle surrounded the cook. They turned to watch as the cook swung the limb like a club, his long hair flinging back and forth as he flailed away.

"Samson," shouted his father, starting his way down the hill again.

"Oh, no, mon," said the cook. "I don't need your help. Stay with the young ones. Samson can take care of himself."

The burly cook with the blue apron whose front read SAM-SON'S CRAWDAD DINER continued beating the air, occasionally landing a blow to the head of a fleeing cow. He drove the seven into the deepest part of the bog, where they set about a low bellowing as they sank to their deaths. Half an hour later the wind ceased and the humming of insects returned to the once-again peaceful swamp.

"We're fine, Mom. Dad just wanted me to ask you, please, if I can stay over one more night. There's no school tomorrow, and I promise to maybe even clean out my closet when I get home. Please?"

Jacob pumped his fist in the air! Undoubtedly, her answer was "yes." Soon after the ambulance and police left the scene of the year's, possibly the century's, most unusual happening, Jacob, his dad, and Samson sat at a table in the diner.

"Mon oh mon, that was some big seven cows, heh?" asked Samson.

"Biggest seven cows I ever saw," said Jacob.

"Well, the 1963 Texas Longhorns, now those were some big cows, maybe bigger," said Jacob's dad. Everybody laughed for the first time in hours, and when Jacob caught his father's eye, he sported his biggest smile of the year.

On the way back to Orange, his dad reached across the seat and pulled Jacob close to him while he drove. "I was pretty scared there for a few minutes," he said.

"Not me," said Jacob.

"Oh no?"

"Nope. Well, okay, maybe for a few minutes. But once I saw that Samson still had his long hair, I knew he couldn't lose."

They drove in silence for a few miles, till Jacob's dad said, "I'm proud of you, son."

"Thanks, Dad. How come?"

"I see you are keeping up with your reading."

"Sure am, Dad. Every Wednesday night, a chapter a week, just like we used to do." Though neither Jacob nor his dad lived in a perfect world, they both knew it would be a better world come morning, a world without the screaming banshee cattle of the night swamp.

The Chupacabra and Berto

Berto loved his *abuelos,* his grandparents. He loved his
summers spent at the home of his abuelos. Even the
fear of a prowling creature living in the brush behind
their house, a creature who lived on the blood of its victims,
wasn't going to change that. But after his abuelo described in
gory detail *his* encounter with the Chupacabra, Gilbert did stay
closer to home, especially after dark.

Berto spent every summer with his grandparents in the Rio
Grande Valley. They lived in a small town forty miles north of
Laredo. His abuelos were elderly and had a small ranch with
twenty-eight chickens, ten goats, and three fat and lazy milk
cows. Their house was old and made of pine. Once painted

white, it now sprouted gray splinters, like a balding old man with strands of graying hair.

Cactus plants surrounded a large back porch. Some grew in colorful pots from Mexico. Others stuck their prickly arms over the porch from a weedy flower bed below. A swing hung from two thick ropes, and a small mesquite wood table welcomed everyone to enjoy the shaded porch.

In the Rio Grande Valley, the morning sun was especially blistering. Berto always stayed inside the house, helping his grandmother cook their breakfast of corn tortillas, *jamón,* and *huevos con frijoles.* Following breakfast, he helped his grandfather feed the livestock and milk the cows.

One morning, when he was six, his grandfather said, "Berto, maybe feeding the chickens can be your job." So every morning Berto tossed hard corn kernels to hungry chickens, squawking and clucking and scrambling at his feet. After lunch Berto was free to wander and walk through the thick groves of mesquite trees and cacti.

"Always be home before dark!" his *abuela* warned him, at least once a day.

Berto knew of the usual dangers: rattlesnakes, scorpions, and coyotes. He had even heard of other, darker dangers: the Weeping Woman, graveyard ghosts, and the *tecolote* witch owls. But Berto had never heard of the danger feared most by the people of the Rio Grande Valley, the Chupacabra.

One afternoon, when he was ten, Berto grew bored with his chores. As soon as the chickens were fed, he filled his backpack with rolled-up tortillas and a bottle of fresh water. Eager to explore, he hurried to the mesquite brush and dry gullies on the far edge of the ranch. When the sun was high overhead, he sat in the shadows of a rock overhang and ate his lunch of tortillas and gulped down the bottle of water. He then curled up and fell asleep.

An hour later, Berto awoke to a soft rattling sound two feet behind him. He slowly rolled down the gully wall, glancing back to see the thick coils and dancing fangs of a diamondback rattlesnake. Once safe, Berto ran as fast as he dared, dodging cacti and thorny-branched mesquite trees.

Lifting his arm to brush aside a tree branch, he didn't see the rock at his feet. He stumbled and landed facedown, tearing his sleeves at the elbows and skinning his knees. When he finally caught his breath and wiped the tears from his cheeks, Berto climbed the gully wall. He stood on a sandstone boulder to see how far he was from his *abuelo*'s house. At least a mile, he guessed.

"I must not be on abuelo's ranch anymore," he said to himself. He spotted a water tank another half mile away, with a hawk circling overhead. "Gotta see that up close," he said, "and refill my water bottle while I'm at it."

Soon he was leaning over the water tank wall, filling his bottle and splashing water on his face. The hawk flew away, but Berto scanned the blue sky till he once again saw it, this time diving fast.

"Looks like he's spotted a rabbit," said Berto, dashing to see the struggle of hunter and prey. When he reached the site of the hawk's final dive, he stopped and stared at the scene before him. Berto expected to see the hawk holding down the struggling rabbit and clawing through the skin to reach the meat.

The rabbit, true enough, was still as death, twisted and torn. But the hawk lay unmoving as well, facedown in a circle of scattered feathers. Berto heard a rustling in a mesquite tree behind him. He turned to see what looked like a coyote running through the thick underbrush. He returned his gaze to the rabbit and hawk. Picking up a dry sage bush, he poked the animals. Nothing moved.

If they are dead, he thought, *where is the blood?* Not a single drop of blood dotted the ground around the dead hawk and rabbit.

Berto had never witnessed anything like this. He spent the remainder of the day climbing up and down the gully walls. When the sun began to set, he realized he was several miles from his abuelo's house.

Rattlesnakes hunt in the cool of the early evening, Berto knew. He also knew the danger of cacti, mesquite, and unexpected sinkholes in the dry earth. So he made his way very slowly to the house lights. When he reached the porch, his grandmother was there, upset and crying.

"I was so afraid you were hurt," she said. "I almost called your mother to tell her you were missing."

"Please don't do that," said Berto. "She would come and get me, and I don't want to go home yet."

"Oh, mi hijo! I was so afraid."

"I was playing in the brush behind the house," Berto said.

"But after dark! You know we always tell you to be home before dark," his grandmother replied.

"I am sorry. I won't do it again, I promise."

"Come here," she said, and wrapped her arms tight around him. "We were so scared for you." Berto had never seen his abuela cry and carry on so. His grandfather stood silently and watched.

After supper, Berto's abuelo finally spoke. "Let us sit on the back porch, and I will tell you a story."

Berto sat on the swing and his abuelo pulled a chair beside

him. "As you have heard, my father and his brother owned this land, as far as you can see. They had a herd of sheep, goats, and almost a hundred head of cattle. In those days everyone worked on the ranch, even young children. We herded and helped with the branding and did things only grown-ups do today.

"When I was your age, I had my own horse. One evening, in the middle of birthing season when all the workers are very busy, a lamb wandered away from her mother. You could hear her bleating in the darkness. My father told me to find the lamb, to follow her cries and return her to the corral. My uncle gave me a saddle blanket and a rope.

"'Wrap her up in this blanket,' he said. 'Tie one end of the rope around the blanket and the other end to your saddle horn. Ride slowly and drag the lamb behind you.'

"I felt very grown-up and important. I leapt on my horse and rode in the direction of the lamb's cries. In less than half an hour I located the lamb. I was small, but I was a strong boy, much like yourself.

"The lamb's leg was bleeding. She had caught herself under a sharp rock. When she struggled, the rock left a deep gash in her leg. She was unable to walk. I packed earth on the wound to slow the bleeding and wrapped her in the blanket. I tied the rope and began the walk home. My horse was like a friend to me, and very smart. He seemed to know what was required, a slow and steady pace.

"I was close to the circle of lantern lights from the barn, when suddenly my horse stopped. I patted his neck and said, '¡Vaya! Let's go,' but he refused to move. '¡Vaya!' I said again, and this time he did move, but very slowly.

"I knew we had caught on something and I climbed down to take a look. The lamb had stopped crying, but I could see her wriggling and moving beneath the blanket. At least I thought it was the lamb. In truth, the lamb was dead. What I saw moving beneath the blanket was the thing most feared by myself, your grandmother, and all who live in the dry country of the Rio Grande Valley.

"I untied the blanket and flung it open. Two dark eyes glared up at me, shining and reflecting the moonlight. The thing was hideous, a thin and mangy wolflike animal with sharp bloody teeth. It hissed at me like a viper. The lamb's throat was torn open, but no blood flowed from the wound, only from the mouth of the thing, the Chupacabra.

"Grandson, I am lucky to be alive. The Chupacabra was twice my size. He could have leapt upon me. They could have found me lying next to the lamb, dead from the one who kills and eats the blood. Maybe he was no longer hungry. I do not know. I ran with all the speed I had within me.

"Help me!' I called out. '¡Ayúdame!'

"What is it?' asked my uncle.

"The lamb is dead. Cómo lobo, pero no lobo,' I stammered. 'Like a wolf, but not a wolf.'

"I pointed to the brush and fell into the arms of my father, shaking and sobbing. My uncle and four workers grabbed lanterns and rifles and soon were riding toward the Chupacabra. An hour later, after much hollering and gunfire, the men returned.

"They carried nothing, no lamb, no blanket, no Chupacabra. No one said a word. My father turned to my mother and said, 'Take the boy inside. Light a candle and be thankful we are all alive.'

"The next morning I learned they had wrapped the lamb in the blanket and buried her, far away from the ranch. They did this in case the Chupacabra returned for what remained of her.

"So, my grandson, when we tell you to stay close to the ranch and be home before dark, there is a very good reason. That reason still lives in the gullies and mesquite groves of the Rio Grande Valley. Now that you know what he is, you never want to see him. He is the Chupacabra."

Berto never told his abuelo that he had already seen the Chupacabra. That very day, he saw him.

Catfish and the Owl

No matter where you are or how much you think you know, it's always good to have friends who know more. Bobby learned that lesson the hard way. Bobby lived in Tyler, in an old neighborhood near the high school. The houses were wooden rather than brick, and the neighbors were from everywhere.

Diversity?

Bobby knew all about diversity. He lived in it. On his street alone lived families from Vietnam, Mexico, India, the Philippines, and even a sweet older lady from someplace called Cajun Country. One afternoon she even tried to give him *some good ol' Cajun snackfood*. She called it "boo-dan." It looked like sausage to him, but he didn't care what it was. With a name like boo-whatever, he wasn't about to eat it. He had heard about Hansel and Gretel and wasn't about to fall for that one.

The most normal and American of all the families in Bobby's neighborhood was the Bryant family. The parents had moved to Tyler from Idabell, Oklahoma, just a few years ago. When he wasn't in his own driveway shooting baskets, Bobby was almost always in the Bryants' backyard, tossing a football or wrestling with his best friend, Catfish. That wasn't his real name, of course, but everybody called him that.

One day Bobby and Catfish wandered farther away from home than usual. They were tossing the football from one side of the street to the other, and after an hour found themselves in the thick woods surrounding the old high school. They settled on a park bench and watched some bigger boys play basketball. They were strong and quick and sometimes hung on the rim after a basket.

"Wow!" said Catfish. "These guys are good."

"Yeah. I'll bet they could beat the Dallas Mavericks," Bobby said. They both laughed. Up and down the court the young men ran, dribbling hard and soaring to the basket.

The sun dipped below the Tyler skyline, and Bobby said, "Guess we'd better head home." They stood to go, but a rustling sound from the leaves above made them stop. Squirrels ran and tussled all day long in these trees, but this sound was different. It started as a shrill chirping, like squirrels make, but what followed froze them in their tracks.

A long and low sound, deeper than the wind, shivered the leaves. They looked above their heads and saw an enormous owl. It cast its eyes in their direction, then unfolded the largest wings Bobby had ever seen and flew away.

Catfish didn't hesitate.

"Come on!" he shouted. "We need to get home!"

"Wait!" said Bobby. "Look at the size of that owl. It's coming back. I want to see it." The owl circled the playground and settled in the thick foliage of a red oak tree.

Catfish was already half a block away and running like his life depended on it. Bobby picked up the football and, tossing it to himself, made his way to the red oak. He shaded his eyes from the late afternoon sun and looked for the owl.

"Hello, young man," a voice came from behind him. Bobby was startled and dropped the football. He turned to see an elderly woman wearing a ragged maroon sweater with holes at both elbows. Her face was thin; her nose was flat and broad. The woman was dark-skinned and her hair, though she stooped with age, was shiny and black.

"Uh. Hello," said Bobby.

"Where did your friend go?" the woman asked.

"Well, we saw an owl and I think it scared him. He ran home. At least I think he did."

"Too bad," said the woman. "We could play some games."

"Games?" said Bobby, and the tilt of his head made the old woman laugh.

"Oh," she said, when she finished laughing. "I guess I do look too old and frail for football. Well, I don't mean football. Other games," she said, pointing to the gate of the nearby graveyard. Sycamore trees sagged and surrounded the cemetery, their branches hanging over the fence and touching the ground.

"Yeah, maybe some other time," said Bobby. "I better be going." He picked up the football, but when he turned to say good-bye, the woman was gone.

Bobby heard a rustling in the treetop. The owl looked down

at him, flapping its wings in slow motion and lifting its legs from the branch before it flew in the direction of the graveyard.

When Bobby entered his living room, his mom folded her arms and looked at her watch. "Pretty late to be out playing, don't you think?"

"Yeah. I'm sorry." Bobby tossed the football on the sofa. "We went to the park and watched some basketball players."

"Catfish called while you were gone," his mother said. "He asked if you could have supper with his family tonight. I told him all right, but it is a school night, so be home by seven thirty."

"Cool! Can I go now?"

"Fine with me. Just be home on time."

Bobby soon stood on the Bryants' front porch, ringing the doorbell. Catfish answered. He didn't even say hello, just waved his arm for Bobby to enter.

"We're eating on the back porch tonight," he said.

During the supper of corn soup and frybread, which Bobby knew from a powwow at the college, everyone sat quietly.

"Would you like some honey, Bobby?" Catfish's mother asked. Bobby nodded yes and doused his frybread with thick amber honey.

They asked me over to tell me something, Bobby thought. As soon as everyone finished eating, Catfish's father turned to Bobby.

"I don't know if Catfish told you that we are Choctaws," he said. "Our ancestors walked on the Trail of Tears. We are Americans, but we are also Oklahoma Choctaws."

"Okay," said Bobby. "No, he never told me."

"Well, there is no reason he would. At least not until now. Catfish had some trouble in Oklahoma we think you should know about. He was playing football one Saturday, and there was a fight after the game. Bobby hit another boy and bloodied his nose."

Bobby looked at Catfish, but Catfish had his head down, looking ashamed. "I never saw Catfish hit anybody," said Bobby.

"Well, boys fight all the time," said his father, "but this time it was different. The boy's grandmother was very angry and came over to our house that night. She wanted to talk to Catfish by himself. When I wouldn't allow that, she grew even angrier. 'I have friends,' she shouted. 'You will be sorry, and so will your mean little boy!' After she left we watched television and went to bed, like every other evening."

"That night we heard a clawing sound on the roof of our house. I took my shotgun outside and saw a large owl scratching at the shingles on the roof. He had already torn several shingles and seemed to be trying to enter the house. I fired the shotgun and the owl flew away."

At that moment the shrill cry of an owl rang loud and long, coming from an elm tree in the creek behind the house.

"Let's go inside!" said Catfish's dad. His voice was loud and nervous. Bobby picked up a plate to help clear the table, but the Bryants seemed in a hurry to get inside. Catfish gently pushed him through the patio door.

"We'll clean up tomorrow," he said. Bobby was frightened by how strange everyone was acting. He followed Catfish and his family to the living room. Bobby sat on the carpeted floor with the Bryant brothers, Catfish, Kenny, and Billy, and the parents settled on the sofa.

"Bobby, you must be very careful in the days ahead," continued Catfish's father. "Stay close to home and don't go out after dark, not even in your backyard. The owl has found Catfish."

Hearing this, Catfish's mother took her husband's hand. Kenny and Billy scooted closer to Catfish, as if to protect him.

"Not long after the playground fight," Mr. Bryant continued, "Catfish had his first nosebleed. It started as a tiny spot of blood on his pillow. His mother spotted it one morning after Catfish had left for school. That same school day, while the children were outside during recess, Catfish felt a trickle of blood running down his face. He told his teacher, who tried to stop the flow with a handkerchief. She took Catfish to the nurse, but the bleeding wouldn't stop."

"The nurse called me at work, and I drove Catfish to the emergency room at the hospital, and only the doctors were able to stop the blood flow."

Catfish turned his head away, embarrassed that Bobby now knew his secret. Bobby was just about to say something, when the owl screeched, louder than before, echoing through the house. But the owl was not crying the usual cry of an owl.

"Catfish!" the owl seemed to say, in a deep and vibrating voice. "Caa-aa-aa-aa-tuh Feeeeeee-shush!"

Mr. Bryant first ran to the back door and locked it.

"Don't move," he said quietly over his shoulder. While Mr. Bryant stepped quickly through the house, locking and testing every door and window, Mrs. Bryant turned off the lights and pulled the curtains closed.

Once the house was darkened and tightly locked, Mr. Bryant relaxed. He served Cokes to the boys and made a pot of coffee for himself and his wife, served by the light of a tiny lamp in the center of the table. "Okay, we need to get some sleep," he soon declared, and Bobby said his good-byes.

"I'll walk you home," said Mr. Bryant.

The next day Catfish wasn't at the bus stop, and when Bobby knocked on the Bryant front door after school, nobody answered. He dribbled his basketball on the sidewalk for over an hour, waiting.

"Bobby," his mother called. "I need your help." While Bobby carried the kitchen trash out, he heard the phone ring. When he returned, his mother was ending a short conversation, saying, "I'll tell him now. Thanks for calling."

"Who was that?" Bobby asked.

"That was Mr. Bryant. He said to tell you they have gone to Idabell for a few days."

"Why?"

"He said they were going to speak to the grandmother of a friend of Bobby's, someone he got in a fight with. He said you would understand."

"Oh," said Bobby. "Okay. Yeah, that makes sense. They're trying to patch things up."

"In the middle of the week? Seems like they could have waited till the weekend."

"Well, some things just can't wait," said Bobby, slipping outside before his mother could find something else for him to do. He wiggled under the loose wire of the back fence and sat on a log by the creek. The creek water was low and barely flowing. Storm clouds were gathering overhead, and a cool breeze chilled his cheeks and ears. Bobby shivered.

He never heard the woman, the woman from the playground, walk up behind him. He never felt the log move when she sat next to him, but when she spoke, Bobby was so startled he fell backward off the log.

"Hello." That's all she said, and when he regained his seat she pointed to his house and asked, "Do you live there?"

"Uh-huh," Bobby nodded, then wished he had lied.

"Your little friend lives next door," she said.

"I have to go," Bobby said, and as he dove under the fence he heard leaves rattling in an elm tree. "Please," he whispered to himself. "No."

His greatest fear was answered. Bobby heard the long cry of the owl, and when he looked to the sound the owl stared at him, as if to say, "I will be back."

After supper Bobby started his math homework, but the written problems all seemed to pose the same question.

Where is Catfish?

At ten o'clock, he heard the Bryants' car in the driveway. He dashed through the living room, where his parents were watching CNN news, and called over his shoulder as he ran out the front door, "Going to see Catfish! Be right back." But something about the way the wind picked up the moment he left his front porch told him he would not return home anytime soon.

Trees shook in the sudden heavy wind, with an ear-splitting whooshing noise. Bobby watched as Mrs. Bryant half-carried Catfish to the house, while Mr. Bryant hurried the brothers from the car. The last he saw of Catfish, his mother was wrapping a thick towel around his head. As she fumbled with the house keys, the towel dropped to the porch. It was soaked in fresh blood. *Catfish's blood,* thought Bobby.

Bobby took a step in the direction of the Bryant house, then thought better of it and turned toward his own, when a bolt of lightning struck the oak tree between the two houses. A lower branch ripped from the tree and fell on the Bryants' car, smashing the windshield. For a split second the entire street lit up as if a spotlight from the sky shone down. Thunder shook the houses.

Bobby ran to his front door and leapt to the porch. Another clap of thunder shattered the picture window three feet in front of him. He fell backward down the steps and rose from the side-walk running. A flash of lightning cut the night sky and Bobby dove beneath the nearest front porch he could find.

He rolled against a cinder block support, breathing hard and sorting through a world of dark and bloody images. The lightning soon ceased and the wind settled into a sporadic stirring of limbs and tall yard grasses. Bobby crawled from under the porch and stood slowly, peering up and down the street for any sign of danger.

"Finally decide you want some boudin?" Bobby turned to see the old woman from Cajun Country standing behind him. "What's the matter, 'gator got your tongue?" she said, laughing at her own joke.

Bobby shook his head, but once he started shaking, he couldn't stop. Harder and harder he shook, as if everything from the past few days could be shaken away. When he came to his senses, Bobby was sobbing. The woman sat on her porch steps and held Bobby close while he cried like a child half his age.

"My name is Miss Jolie," she finally said, "and I already know who you are, Bobby. Wait right here and I'll bring you something good." Over two cups of steaming dark chocolate, four brownies, and his first taste of Cajun Country boudin, Bobby told Miss Jolie everything he knew about his Choctaw neighbors and the owl woman.

She sat without moving till he sighed and looked at her for help. For the first time, Bobby looked at Miss Jolie's skin. It was thin and soft brown, like chocolate cake icing.

"Running's not gonna solve anything," she told him. "You can't outrun the owl. You can only face it."

"I'm not strong enough," he said.

"Not by yourself you're not. But you're a good kid, Bobby.

I've watched you grow up. This neighborhood has changed, but you don't care what language anybody speaks or where their folks are from. You're friendly with everybody. Not all the kids are, you know."

Bobby listened. "There is always help for the good," Miss Jolie said. "Let's go inside and see what we can find." Bobby followed her into a carpeted living room with a sofa and two comfy chairs.

"Have a seat," she said, and disappeared down a hallway. Bobby studied the soft yellow wallpaper and baby-blue window curtains. *Like my grandmother's,* he thought.

Miss Jolie returned with a leather bag. "Bobby," she said, "a Choctaw friend of mine once gave me a gift you might need." Bobby's eyes grew big.

"What? You think you're the only one with Choctaw friends?" Miss Jolie said. "Truth is, I'm part Choctaw myself. There's lotsa Choctaws in Louisiana. Mississippi, too. Yes, I am part Choctaw, part African-American, part Cajun French, and all-the-way American!"

"Me, too," said Bobby, smiling for the first time in hours. "Well, the last part, the all-the-way American part!" Miss Jolie's bright green eyes beamed. She reached into the bag and from it pulled a large gray-brown feather.

"It is an owl feather, Bobby, and I want to give it to you." His eyes grew big and he took a step away.

"Well," she said, "you are right to be cautious. But this owl feather will protect you, not harm you. A wing feather from an owl will repel any other owl and remove her power over you."

"I should give this feather to Catfish," said Bobby. "He needs it more than I do."

Miss Jolie smiled. "That thinking is exactly why you are going to win, Bobby. You think about others before yourself."

She reached in the bag and pulled out another feather.

"Here's a feather for Catfish," she said. "For now, why don't you and Catfish carry the feathers in your shirt pockets, over your hearts. Catfish'll get better just by having the feather, at least for a few days."

"Then what?" asked Bobby.

"Then that owl will make one final try for Catfish. You need to stay close to him. And Bobby?"

"Yes."

"Stay in the light as much as possible. The light is your friend. You should be going home now. Your parents are worried."

"OK," said Bobby, rising to go. "Thank you, Miss Jolie."

As Bobby stepped outside he glanced to the sky. The moon was already twinkling through fast-moving clouds.

"Now where is that cane?" Miss Jolie asked herself, once Bobby was gone. She rummaged through a bedroom closet till she found a crooked cedar cane. A long grey feather hung from the handle. "I knew you'd come in handy someday," she said, and the feather twisted in reply. She smiled, remembering a Cajun Choctaw from years ago, the man who'd given her the cane.

Bobby's parents met him at the door and he told them of being almost blown away. "But I'm safe now," he said. "The lady from Cajun Country took me in till the storm blew over."

"Miss Jolie?" asked his mother.

"Yes," said Bobby. "How did you know her name?"

"Oh, Bobby, everybody knows Miss Jolie. I'll bet she fed you boudin. She makes the best!"

"It was the best boo-dan I ever had!" Bobby agreed.

The next morning, while city workers cleaned tree limbs and blown-about debris from the neighborhood, Bobby rode to school with the Bryants.

"No need to keep any secrets from you, now, Bobby," said Mr. Bryant. "We visited with the family of the boy in Idabell. Seems the grandmother died not long after we left, so we couldn't patch things up with her. At first no one knew, or admitted knowing, who the witch might be."

"But as we were leaving, the teenage brother followed us to the car. He said there was an old woman who hadn't been seen in a month. Newspapers cluttered her front yard, and not even kinfolks would step foot on her place. When I asked him where she lived, he said, 'If you came here to make things better for your son, stay away from that rundown house.' He said it was evil and so was the woman who lived there."

Bobby told about Miss Jolie and showed Catfish and his dad the owl feathers.

"Well," said Mr. Bryant, "she seems to know something about witches. Just be careful, boys, and stay together."

The next two days passed without incident. The afternoon of the third day, Bobby took Catfish to the creekside log. *Running's not gonna solve anything. You can't outrun it, you can only confront it*, he remembered Miss Jolie saying.

Five minutes after they sat down, the owl appeared, settling in a sycamore tree overhanging the creek. She flapped her wings in slow motion till she had the boys' attention. Then, with claws outstretched, she dove for Catfish. The young Choctaw boy covered his face and leapt behind the log.

"Your feather, Catfish! Show her your feather!" shouted Bobby. But the owl had already landed on Catfish and gripped his right hand in her claws. Catfish shook his hand free and blood splattered on the surrounding bushes.

As Bobby later told the story, seeing his own blood seemed to strengthen Catfish, not scare him. He swatted the powerful bird away from his face and stood strong, taking the feather from his pocket and waving it at the bird.

As if in league with the owl, the wind swirled and howled, knocking limbs from trees and preventing the boys from climbing out of the creek bed. Rain pelted them, thick cold raindrops falling from a darkened sky. The owl flew backward for a moment, then circled the boys and launched her attack from behind them, swooping and clawing at their heads. Their eyes were blinded by the rain, and Bobby realized they could not hold her off.

Just as suddenly as it had arisen, the wind ceased. The light returned, and once-evil raindrops now sparkled from yellow sycamore leaves. The owl lay on the log, staring at the air with unseeing eyes. Her right wing hung loose and broken at her side.

Catfish smiled and Bobby followed his gaze. Miss Jolie stood holding her cane, looming over the scene. Larger than the log she stood, larger than the boys, and so much larger than the owl woman, who now took on her human form and sat on the log, breathing hard and looking at the three.

"You have done your damage, more to yourself than anyone else," said Miss Jolie to the owl woman. "It is time for you to find your way home, where your strength lies. Blessings on your journey." The owl woman limped to the creek bed and vanished in the red oak woods.

Bobby never forgot the lessons of those growing-up days in

Tyler. He learned that good is truly stronger than evil, and that evil thrives in darkness. For the remainder of his days, he and Catfish strove to live in the light.

As for the owl woman, she already knew these lessons. She merely moved to new places of darkness, till later years. Once she found the path of goodness and walked upon it, the circle of her days came never to an end.

Two Graves

September 27, 2004. Gene stood in the drizzle and wished he'd worn his boots instead of his basketball shoes on his first official night as a runaway. He stood before an iron fence encircling a deserted house, a once regal two-story house with all the windowpanes broken.

"There's got to be a lot of glass on the floors," he said to himself. "I should have worn my boots."

Gene pushed open the gate and stopped. Just to the right of the entryway lay a cobblestone path, leading to a small knoll topped by a grove of elm trees. Following the path, he entered a tiny family graveyard with only two tombstones. One tombstone was clearly marked as the grave of ROBERT MATHESON.

The other stone was bare, as if awaiting a beloved.

Gene retraced his steps and approached the front porch, a dilapidated wooden structure sloping to the yard. He felt the sadness of the house wash over him as his foot touched the first of three steps, testing to see if the warped boards would support him. The screen door creaked, beating back and forth in the night breeze. It hung crookedly, held to the frame by a single bottom hinge. Gene pushed the door aside and reached for the doorknob. He paused and, out of habit, knocked.

He half expected a porch light to come on and someone from inside to yell, "Go away! We're trying to sleep in here! Come back in the morning."

When no one did, he turned the knob and entered the house. He was greeted by a wide hallway leading to a stairway and rooms to the right and left. Gene heard the steady beat of rain on the roof and the heavy dripping of a leak coming from the room to his right. He turned to the opposite room and was pleased to see the remains of an old sofa near a stone fireplace. The stuffing was strewn about the floor, but the sofa seemed warm and welcoming.

Gene had walked almost eight miles since crawling through his bedroom window, and he was both hungry and tired. He felt the sofa for rats, scorpions, or rattlesnakes. Finding none, he grabbed a sheet from the room's large window and sank into the center cushion for a short nap. The first indication that this night would be the most frightening of Gene's life came with a sound, a soft shuffling sound behind him. Someone was crossing the floor and approaching him.

He slowly turned. Floating in the air, less than a foot from his face, were the hands of an elderly man. The fingers had chipped, brown fingernails and swollen knuckles. Gene saw no arms or body, only the hands.

He stared at the hands, unable to move. A skinny finger

moved closer and closer. Gene was hypnotized by the trembling of the hand and the slow unfolding of the palm, revealing a gold ring with a small red ruby.

When the finger touched his chin, Gene lunged backward. The rotting floorboards gave way and he fell to the basement below. He grabbed the air and flailed his arms before landing on a tow sack of old corn husks.

Gene lay on his back for several minutes, his eyes wide open and his chest heaving. When he settled into the realization that he had stopped falling and suffered no broken bones, he felt the back of his head. A large bump was tender to his touch.

"Owww!" he said and grimaced in pain. Gene stood up and looked for a door or window. A flight of stairs led to the ground floor. He climbed carefully up to the beckoning door. The steps creaked, and he tried each one with a testing foot.

The door was locked, bolted, or nailed from the other side. Gene was not surprised. He retreated to the basement and searched the walls for a window or any access to the outside. Night was falling, and he did not relish the idea of his first night away from home spent in the basement of a haunted house. He had no doubt, in spite of what his parents and teachers would tell him, this *was* a haunted house.

He hoped for a ladder, but of course there was none. Gene settled for a chair, a rickety wooden chair with a seat of woven cane. His grandmother had a set of similar chairs from the 1920s.

I hope this is stronger than that old chair, he thought, remembering how he had fallen through the cane when he tried to change a lightbulb.

He dragged the chair beneath the splintered floorboards, hanging dangerously ten feet over his head. Had he been thinking clearly, he would have known not to try it. But the sun was sinking fast, the light was almost gone, and he had seen a ghost for the first time in his life. How could he be thinking clearly?

Gene reached his full height, aiming for the thickest and sturdiest-appearing board, but it hovered two feet beyond his fingertips. He tried standing on his toes, then jumping. The cane gave way and he fell through the chair and to the floor. With no corn sacks to break his fall, he landed hard on his shoulder and felt the rise of a painful bruise.

He was wrestling himself from the broken chair when he felt a damp spot on the seat of his britches. In the dying light, he saw water seeping through cracks in the wall, a steady drip-drip-dripping. Puddles formed, and the dripping increased to a faucet-like flow. He heard a splash and turned to see another leak on the opposite wall.

Gene was at first more curious than afraid.

"It must be raining outside," he told himself, hoping. In less than a minute, the walls gave way and a flood of water roared into the basement, picking him up and throwing him against a stack of boxes on the far wall. The boxes tore and spilled unseen remnants of a past life into the violent river.

Gene struggled to stay above the water. It gushed with a power he had never felt, and soon the basement was filled. He tried to swim to the hole in the floor, but the water surged away from the opening.

Only inches of air remained, and Gene realized he would probably drown and maybe never be found, not by his parents, not by his friends. He might be a body forever trapped beneath the debris of this old uninhabited house. No one would ever look for him here. His lungs were burning and he sputtered, splashing and gasping.

Through the murky waters Gene clearly made out the body

of a woman, her eyes closed and her arms and legs hanging limp.

There was a body in the basement! he thought. *The water uncovered a body!* A yellow warning sign floated near the body: DANGEROUS CURVE.

Gene opened his mouth to scream, then wished he hadn't, for he swallowed a mouthful of stale and filthy water. His arms fell, and as he sank, he spotted a large book floating a few feet away, a thick and ancient volume made of leather. Hoping to cling and float on the buoyancy of the book, he reached for it. When his fingers touched the book, the whirling waters stopped.

As suddenly as the water had risen, it now went away. Like a lake that once was and then was no more, the water was gone.

Gene heard a sucking sound and saw the boards return to the walls, and one by one the drops reversed their fall till the basement was dry again. His hair, his clothes, everything was as dry as when he first fell into the space.

Gene lay on his back in the cloud of his fear.

This time when the man's hands appeared in the air in front of him, Gene welcomed them. Any form of humanness was better than the black of being alone and forgotten.

As Gene watched, the old man's hands moved to the book, now lying against the wall. Thin fingers flipped the brittle, crackling pages. Old photographs shone from the pages with a light of their own. The hands disappeared, leaving the book open to a spread of what appeared to be wedding pictures.

Gene rose and stood over the volume. His eyes scanned the pictures, not knowing what he would see that could possibly mean anything to him.

Then he saw it: the ring, the golden ring with one small ruby in the center. Not one ring, but two, sparkled from the page, two gold wedding rings worn by a bride and a groom. The picture displayed two hands, nothing more, two hands gripping a knife and cutting a wedding cake.

Gene stared at the photo. He knew the hand belonged to the old man whose ghost he had seen. He wondered what had happened to his bride. The light waned and his head dropped slowly to his chest. His eyelids grew heavy and he sank to the floor, exhausted by the events of the day, his first day as a runaway, his first day of seeing a ghost. He lay his head on the soft corn husks and fell asleep.

Long after sunrise, Gene awoke to a banging sound coming from the top of the stairs. Light shown through the door. The door was open! He ran to the first floor and sped through the house. He stumbled down the front steps and flung the gate open.

He was about to run in the direction of home when he remembered the graveyard with two tombstones, one unmarked, the other inscribed.

"Robert Matheson," he said aloud. "I spent the night with the ghost of Robert Matheson."

A police car came to a slow halt in front of the house, and a young officer stepped from the car.

"Is your name Gene Hathaway?" he asked. Gene nodded.

"You need to come with me, son. Your parents have spent the night looking for you, along with most of the police force. You've caused quite a bit of trouble."

"Will you take me home?" Gene asked.

"We'll go to the station first, then I'll call your parents."

Gene said not a word as the policeman drove his car away from the decaying structure of the old house. The quickest road to downtown crossed over a dam built fifty years ago across the

Trinity River. A sprawling lake with twenty miles of shoreline now decorated the landscape. As the patrol car eased around a sharp curve, Gene saw the sign, the sign that brushed against the body of the dead woman.

DANGEROUS CURVE

"Stop!" he shouted.

"What is it?" the patrolman asked.

"That sign," Gene said, pointing and nodding his head. For the next twenty minutes Gene told the officer everything he had seen since he left home. The officer listened quietly. When Gene was finished, he sighed.

"When I was about your age," the officer said, "I saw my grandfather a week after his funeral. No one believed me, so be prepared for no one to believe you either."

"Do you believe me?" asked Gene.

"Yes, I do, but I won't make your story part of my official report. Do you understand why?"

"Yes," said Gene. "Just having you not think I am crazy, that's enough."

The officer smiled and patted his shoulder. "Well," he replied, "crazy or not, you do have some problems that need to be worked out with your parents."

"I know," said Gene, "and I feel real sorry about what I've put them through. But would you do me one favor? Would you let me show you what I found in the basement of the old house? An album with pictures of a bride and a groom."

The officer returned with Gene to the Matheson mansion. He found the wedding album and carried it to the station. After a tearful reunion with his parents, and a stern look from his father, Gene asked the officer, "Would you go through old records and see if you can find anything about Mrs. Matheson missing?"

Following an extensive search, it was discovered that Mrs. Matheson had indeed disappeared, less than a year after the wedding. Two days later, Gene and the officer stood on the shore and watched three divers search for the car in the vicinity of the dangerous curve.

Gene had a feeling they would find the car beneath a clump of sycamore trees lining the shore, and his hunch proved to be correct. After thirty minutes of diving, they found the body, in a Buick sedan half-covered in river bottom mud.

Mrs. Matheson was buried on the knoll beside the house. The ceremony was witnessed by only a handful of people, among them the divers, the officer, Gene, and his parents. As far as anyone knew, the couple's friends had all passed away. Afterward, Gene stepped to the porch of the Matheson mansion. He felt a cheerfulness coming from the warped old boards.

Before leaving, he looked through the window at the fireplace. He caught his breath. A fire glowed from the hearth, and standing before it were the Mathesons, pretty and handsome as on their wedding day.

Gene told no one what he saw, nor did he tell what he found in his pocket before going to bed that night: the ring, the golden ring with one small ruby in the center.